Steve Coleman &
Katrina Guazzo

Naree
the Fire Lady

This book is dedicated to you the reader, also to you the attentive listener, the story teller, the artist, the dreamer. In particular, it is dedicated to the medium that dwells within you and within every one of us, bridging the divide between the physical and the imagined, entwining the two into a single braid of creative awe... That primitive energy that has the power to rejuvenate and move whenever we choose to just be still and listen for a while.

Rev. date: 08/29/2013

To order additional copies of this book, contact:
Xlibris LLC
1-800-455-039
www.xlibris.com.au
Orders@Xlibris.com.au

Design/Layout:
Through The Looking Glass Studio
www.looking-glass.com.au

Naree
the Fire Lady

Naree lived with her brothers and sisters by the waterhole with its arching paper barks and turtles and fish in the still, shady water beneath.

The water hole filled up every year after the fires had burned the old grass and the rains had come bringing the earth back to life.

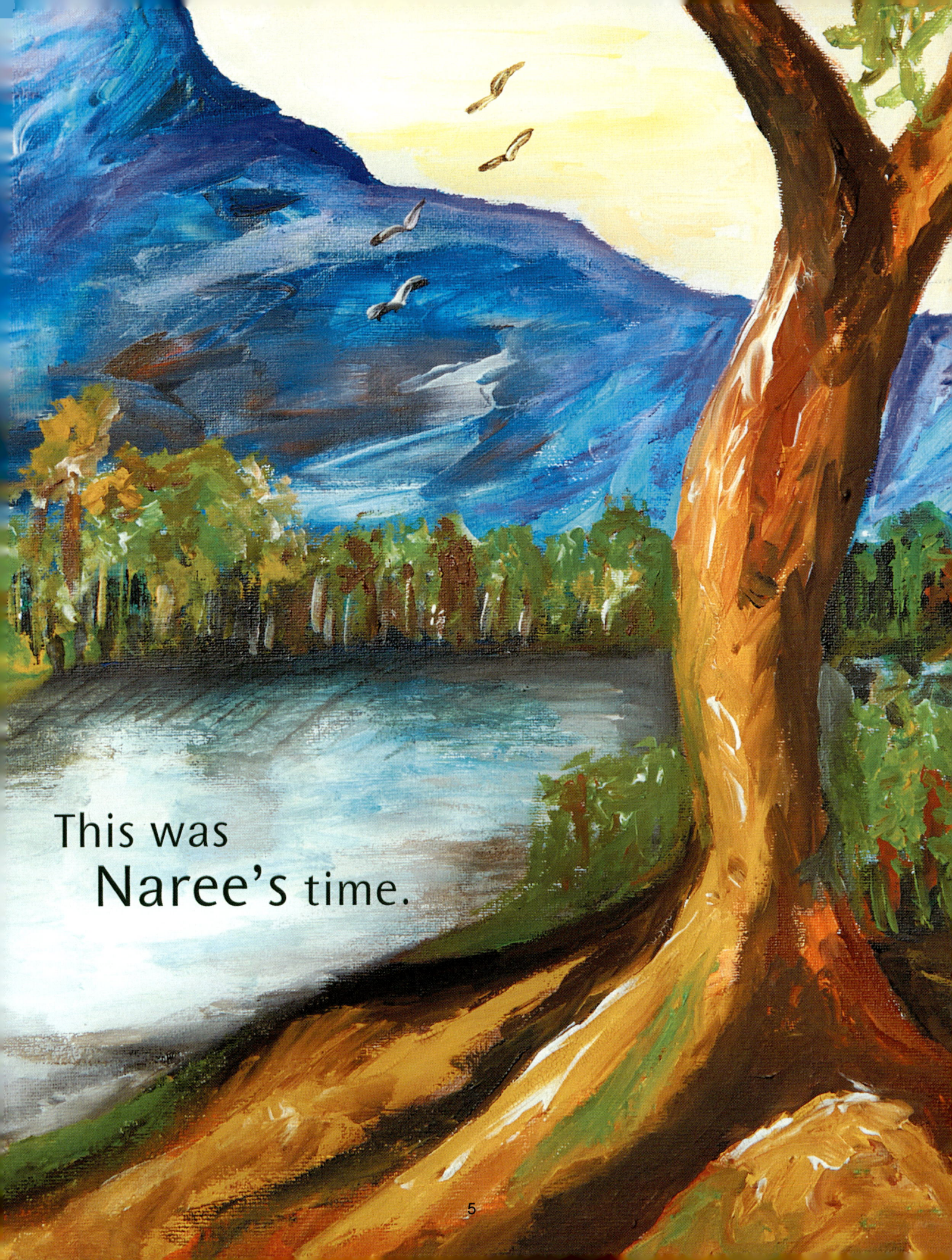

This was
Naree's time.

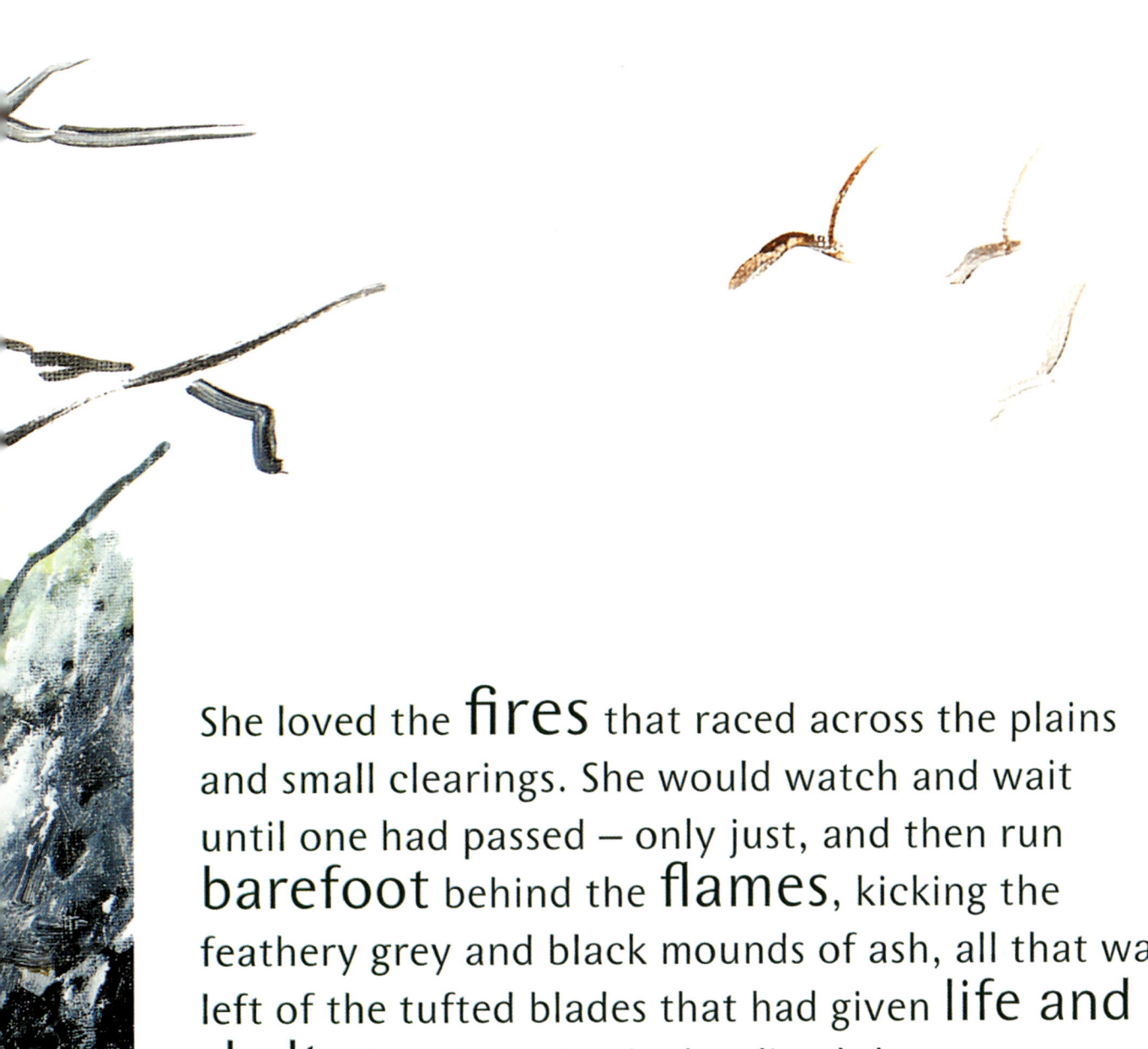

She loved the fires that raced across the plains and small clearings. She would watch and wait until one had passed – only just, and then run barefoot behind the flames, kicking the feathery grey and black mounds of ash, all that was left of the tufted blades that had given life and shelter to the animals that lived there.

Naree would dart nimbly between the smoldering sticks and still burning strips and fragments of bark, all the while leaving her neat foot prints etched into the new mantle of ash – her head band of new, dry leaves and tiny feathers and coloured seeds rising and falling with her long, dark hair as she moved.

When the fire had passed, she would run
to the water hole and slip silently into the
shallows cooling her feet
and soaking up the coolness
of shaded water on her skin.

She would sometimes sit, cross-legged beneath the
surface on the shingle and soft cool mud
holding her breath and with her simple
bush coronet still on her head,
just above the water.

The tiny fish would come, and yabbies and
occasional turtle and listen to Naree tell
them of her life above the water, amongst the
paper barks and on the plains and small clearings
through which she had run.
She would tell them of her family – how they
lived and why they needed to be
near the water hole.

Naree listened also.

The **tiny creatures** and **turtles**
told her of their time in that water,
when all was dry above and waiting
for the next **rain** when the **creek** that
brought new water down from the **hills**
churned and tumbled the pebbles and
sand and heavy sticks into a cloudy
flushing **current**.

It would settle in time with
new life of another year
growing, maturing and
preparing for the **dry season**
that would come soon.

The **kangaroos** would come to drink in the early morning and as the sun set before night. The **dingoes**, at their time in the heat of the afternoon, and the **wild pigs** after dark, digging and turning the banks in order to grow and prepare for their dry and testing time to come.

Naree learned of things past and things yet to come from the **creatures** of that **water**. She would tell her brothers and sisters, and her family and others of what she had learned so that they could be ready themselves for **their time** ahead.

They loved **Naree** and would often quietly sit under the paper barks and watch her as she sat, still and **beautiful** in that water hole.

Seasons came and went by. Naree grew from a little girl. She became lithe and graceful - taller and elegant, yet still nimble and still drawn by the **hot flames** as the fires moved through the **bush** and the clearings of old grass - her head bearing the **symbols of the day past**, rising and falling as she ran ... down to the water hole to sit, still and silent, to listen and to teach and nurture the **creatures of the underworld**.

More people came too – from other places, some even from far away, to quietly watch and listen to **Naree** share her knowledge and wisdom. They called her the **Fire Lady**.

A season came though, when Naree knew she had to go. She knew she had to leave and move away to other parts of the land, to listen in the shallow water holes and to speak and to teach the people who lived there. She would have to leave her brothers and sisters and family .... for ever.

A night came when the moon was down and the bush quiet – no rustles, no feet... no paws shuffling or scurrying. Even the tall wrapped paper barks were silent and still. Naree slipped from her bed. She placed on her head the crown of new leaves and freshly dropped feathers and bush seeds that she had made the day before. She then glided between the long shadows down to the water hole.

Ever so gently she slid into the dark water where she had sat so often, where the turtles and tiny fish had come to share their world and tell Naree their stories. Naree reached up with her hand and pulled from her hair a single small seed. She reached down under the water and pushed the seed into the cool shingle and mud at the bottom of that special place.

Then she left - across the clearings where the fires would soon come and to the water holes across the plains and to the people waiting to listen and to learn of things past and of what was yet to come in that land.

Naree's sisters and brothers came when
the sun was high that morning, down to
the water, to see her yet again.
Her family and others came to see her
beneath the crown of leaves and
feathers and seeds for that new day.

She was not there!

They waited.

She never came.

Her sisters and brothers and family and others came the next day and the next and the next. Naree still didn't come. Soon the people came no more. The fires raced across the clearings and the plains. Her sisters watched, hoping to see Naree nimbly following the flames and running down to the water hole.

Naree never came.
Even when the rains came there was no Naree
sitting in the shallows.
Days went by.
The quiet shade under the paper barks by that
sad and lonely water remained empty.

when the moon was sinking and the bush was quiet and still, something very, very wonderful happened. The night cooled and the sky went light to the east.

Naree's brothers and sisters and others arose from their sleep. They gathered silently and strangely excited..... as if roused by some strange leaping power that danced in their hearts. They knew it was time...... time to make their first walk to the waterhole.... to remember their sister and their daughter and their own wise and truly beautiful Lady of Fire.

They walked to the paper barks on the bank and arrived there as the first rays of the new sun pierced the low clouds and lit up that special place where they had come to remember.

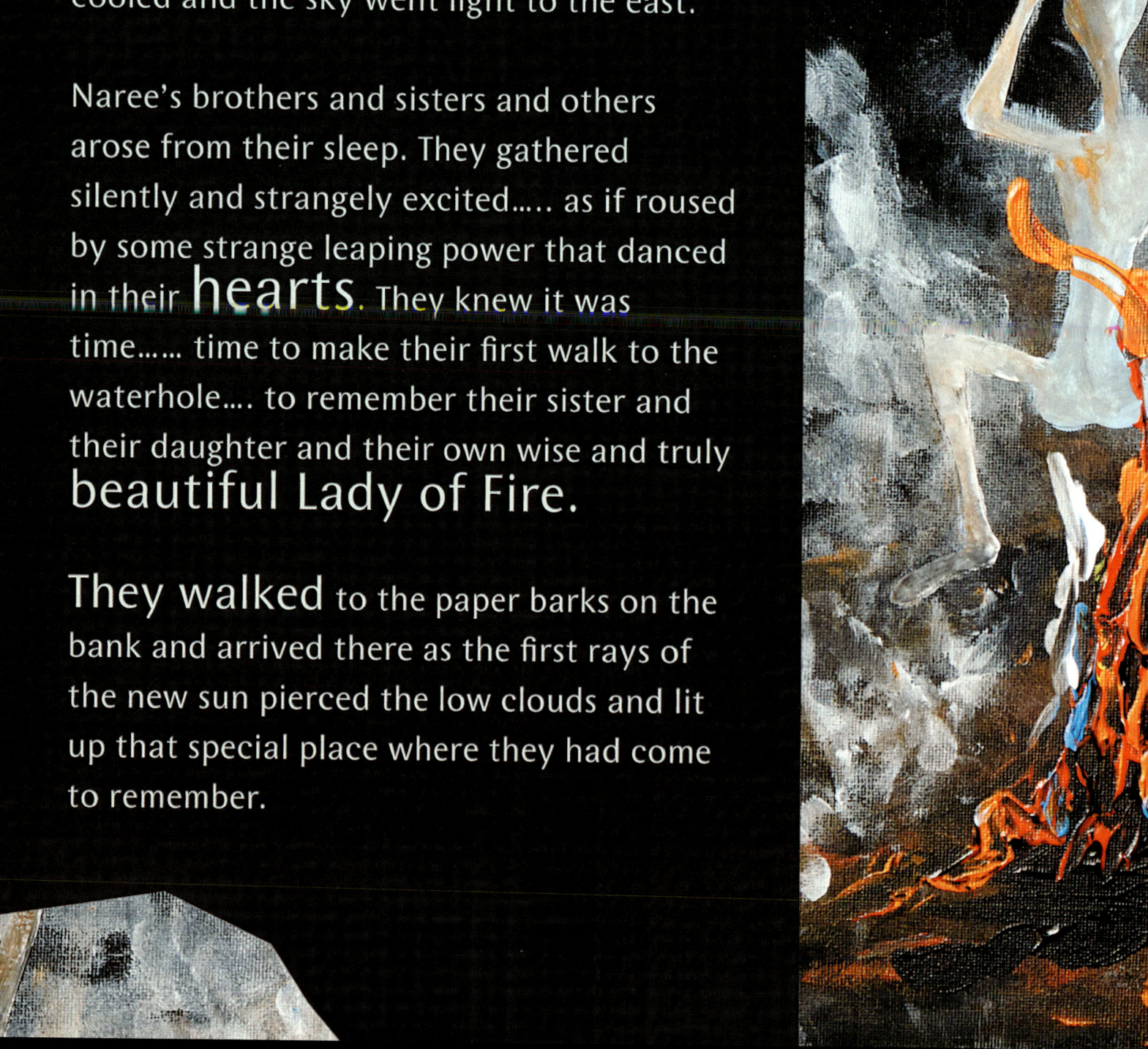

They looked where Naree had sat for them, where the water was just so deep and there, there on the water was a sight they had never seen, in all their time by that water hole.

Spreading out above where Naree had sat, was a large flat and shiny leaf …. floating …. effortlessly. Beside it, at the very spot where Naree's crown of new leaves and feathers and bush seeds had been, was a flower, so beautiful, so magnificent, so clear and whole, so coloured in white and yellow and Orange.

The people stared … in wonder … in amazement. Some felt their hearts beat faster and lift, bringing tears to their early morning eyes.

One cried out, "Naree has returned. She has not forgotten us. She has come back to tell us her stories again." Then silence fell and the people, without words or signal, sat underneath those paper barks and listened. They listened again to Naree's stories of the creatures and the plants of the water… of the animals and birds that lived by that waterhole, and out on the plains and high on the slopes of thick bush where the creek rushed and tumbled and trickled….. and then dried.

She had left them a gift of her knowledge
and her wisdom, wrapped in the colours and
soft perfume of the
first water lily.

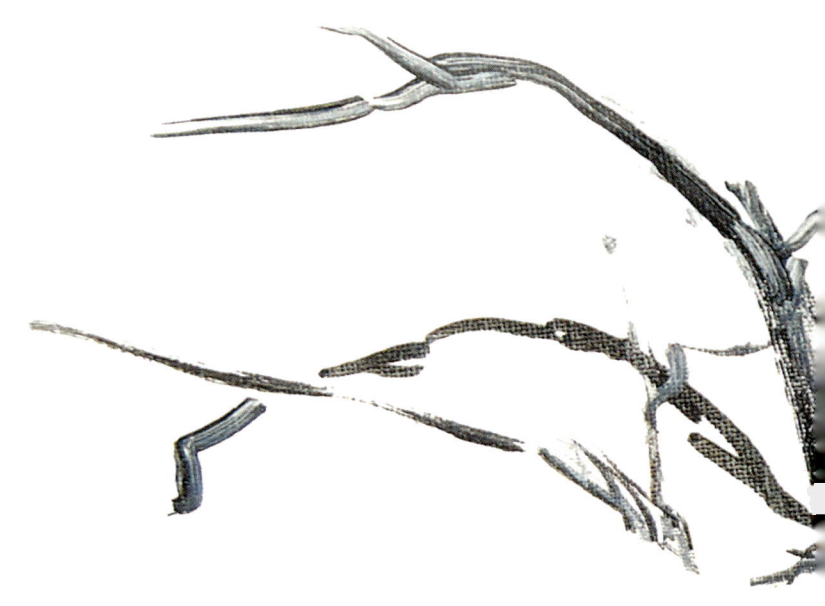

And to **this day**, after the fires have burned across the clearings and the plains, and **the rains** have come and the shingle and mud have settled after the **creek's swift run,** people come to that water hole and sit... quietly ... listening in the **shade of the paper barks**, to Naree... sharing her wisdom and teaching about the water and **the land** and **the fires** that come to burn the old grass ready for a new season.

And **what of Naree, the Fire Lady?**

Naree lives where the **water lilies** are, in every **water hole** across the land, sharing her **magic** and her **beauty** and her stories with anyone who cares to sit **quietly**... under the paper barks

... and listen.

Steve's passion for bush stories grew with him....
from the child of a pioneering community on
Magnetic Island in North Queensland, to his
current profession as a coach, teacher and
mentor based in the great outdoors.
Naree The Fire Lady is one of Steve's many
stories from this personal journey.
To contact Steve, email steve@capabilities21.com

Katrina has loved reading from a young age and
Naree the Fire the Lady enabled her to combine
her passion for painting and books. She works as
a teacher and enjoys painting in her spare time.
This is the first book Katrina has illustrated and
she enjoyed capturing the mystical Naree's beauty
and feminine energy. Katrina lives with her husband
and pets in Townsville, North Queensland, and was
able to gain much inspiration for the illustrations
from her surroundings.
To contact Katrina, email katrina.guazzo@ipc.qld.edu.au

Edwards Brothers Malloy
Ann Arbor MI. USA
June 6, 2017